Lord Kingsdown

Lord Kingsdown's Recollections of his Life at the Bar and in

Parliament

Lord Kingsdown

Lord Kingsdown's Recollections of his Life at the Bar and in Parliament

ISBN/EAN: 9783743337374

Manufactured in Europe, USA, Canada, Australia, Japa

Cover: Foto ©Raphael Reischuk / pixelio.de

Manufactured and distributed by brebook publishing software
(www.brebook.com)

Lord Kingsdown

Lord Kingsdown's Recollections of his Life at the Bar and in Parliament

LORD KINGSDOWN'S

RECOLLECTIONS OF HIS LIFE

AT THE

BAR AND IN PARLIAMENT.

Printed for Perusal by Private Friends only.

1868.

PRINTED BY J. E. TAYLOR AND CO.,
LITTLE QUEEN STREET, LINCOLN'S INN FIELDS.

PREFACE.

Lord Kingsdown, who died at Torry Hill on the 7th October, 1867, told me, on his death-bed, I should find among his papers an imperfect memoir of his early professional life. He prohibited my publishing it; but he did not forbid my showing it to any of his private friends, whom it might interest or amuse, and to any members of his family, to whom it might impart either instruction or amusement.

With a view to such limited circulation,

and for facility of reading, I have caused a few copies only of the following pages to be printed; and I intreat those who receive them to consider them confidential.

EDWARD LEIGH PEMBERTON.

TORRY HILL, *April,* 1868.

Torry Hill, 25th May, 1857.

 HAVE often regretted never having kept a journal in the course of my long life. During the greater portion of it, indeed, I was too much occupied to allow time for the purpose; but when I left the Bar, at Christmas, 1843, I might have begun to do so, and have set down the recollections of an earlier period. It is now too late to repair the neglect: but it may amuse my old age, and form some instruction for any member of my family who may hereafter engage in the same profession with my own, if I note some of the circumstances which have attended a life—for many years—of more uninterrupted prosperity than has often fallen to the lot of man.

B

Its dawn was far from promising so bright a day. My father, who was at the Chancery Bar, died in 1804, at a time when he had attained to very considerable business, but before he had been able to lay by any large sum. I collect from his fee-books that he must have been making about £2000 a year—a good professional income for a junior in Chancery in those days, when fees seem to have been at least a third less in amount than they were in my time. My mother was left with five children, three sons and two daughters, with not more than £500 a year for their support and education, though her income received an augmentation of about £200 a year in 1806, on the death of her parents ; my grandmother surviving her husband only a few months.

My father by his will appointed Mr. Cooke (who had married my mother's sister), together with my mother, guardians of his children. I was eleven years old at his death, and had been sent before I was seven to a large school at Chiswick, kept by Dr. Horne, who had above a hundred scholars, with a view of being transferred to Westminster, and afterwards to Oxford. My mother's scanty income prevented this plan from being carried out. I remained at Chiswick till I was removed from school altogether, at Easter, 1809, when I was but just sixteen. Mr. Farrer, a very old friend of our family, took me into his office for twelve months, at the expiration of which time I went as pupil to my uncle, Mr. Cooke, in whose chambers I remained for five years.

I have frequently considered with myself whether this change in my education tended to my ultimate success or otherwise. At that time nothing but classical literature was taught at public schools ; for this I had always a liking. Mr. Horne, who succeeded his father at Chiswick, was a very good scholar, with the talent, and, unfortunately, with the temper of his family. I had gone through something more than the usual routine of school-books before I left his charge; and when I was my own master, knowing that from my defective education any blunders I might commit would be the more rigorously marked, and my ignorance be held to be even greater than it was, I devoted myself with some assiduity to the study of Greek and Latin authors. I went through Livy, making extracts of passages which seemed to be suited for quotation in public speaking, several pages of which I have lately found, though I do not know that any one of them has ever been turned to account. I went through the Iliad and Odyssey, translating more than one book of the former into Latin hexameters; twice through Thucydides, making an abstract of every passage as I proceeded by a note in the margin; once through Herodotus and Xenophon, and a good many other authors as far as those languages go. Though very far indeed from possessing a competent knowledge of them, I have found in the course of my experience that the greater part of the men with whom I have come in contact have known as little as myself. Living at home with my mother, and studying under my uncle, debarred by poverty from mixing much in society or amusements, I was forced into habits of industry and moral restraint, to which I had from nature but very moderate dispositions.

If, on the other hand, instead of remaining at a private school (of which for a considerable period I was the head, *longo intervallo*), I had gone to Westminster and been knocked about there, and at college, it would perhaps in some degree have cured or diminished the constitutional shyness and timidity which have impeded my progress through life, and prevented me from obtaining, or I should rather say accepting, offices of some consequence in the State. It is possible, however, that if I had been sent to the University my whole course would have been changed. For a great friend of my mother's family, Mr. Wildman, of Chilham Castle, had a good living at his disposal, which my mother fancied he would have given me: and it was not till my success at the Bar had been very great that she was quite reconciled to the supposed loss.

Though probably I might have entered the Church, certainly it would have been from no disposition towards it. Without saying, as I think Cardinal de Retz somewhere observes, that he had "l'âme peut-être la moins ecclésiastique qui fut dans l'univers," I should have felt a strong repugnance to be more than a lay member of the English Church. I was not quite satisfied with its doctrines, and still less with its restraints; and I am thankful that I did not become a member of a profession in which, to an inquiring mind, doubt seems to be inevitable, and in which to doubt must be misery.

The manners and customs of lawyers, or, at least, of Chancery barristers, have so much changed since I became a student —now nearly half a century ago—that it may be worth while to mention Mr. Cooke's habits, which were those of his class. He was regularly at chambers at nine o'clock, remained till past three, dined at four, was at chambers again at six, and stayed till ten. The Chancellor sat from ten till three in his court, at which hour, three times a week during the session of Parliament, he went to the House of Lords and heard appeals till five. The Master of the Rolls sat at six, and continued till ten at night; so that those barristers who were in the first business, especially if they were also in Parliament, had rather a hard time of it. The sittings of the Master of the Rolls, however, were confined to

three nights a week during term. During
the first week after every term he sat of a
morning, the Chancellor's court being ad-
journed, and afterwards every evening
during the intervals between the terms.
He would also come down occasionally to
sit for the Chancellor of a morning, when
he was withdrawn from his court by other
public business.

Always on Saturdays, and generally, I
think, on Sundays, lawyers were engaged
in dinner parties either at home or abroad,
the general hour being half-past five. On
any other day a barrister in any practice, or
ever hoping to acquire any, never for a
moment thought of being away from court
or chambers during the regular hours.
Young men worked harder than it seems
to me to be the fashion to do at present.
While I was at Mr. Cooke's chambers I
plodded regularly through 'Coke upon
Littleton,' making notes as I went along
which filled a pretty thick volume, to say

nothing of Shepherd's 'Touchstone,' and such other light reading. After mastering Fonblanque's 'Treatise of Equity,' I took up the Chancery Reports, and extracted the principles of equity as I found them laid down in Peere Williams (the prince of reporters) and in Vesey's reports of the decisions of Lord Eldon and Sir William Grant. It is a curious proof of the little estimation in which Lord Erskine was held as Chancellor that Mr. Cooke advised me to miss the 13 Ves., in which his judgments are contained.

I am not sure, however, that my legal education, though long and laborious, was by any means successful. My uncle, though an excellent commercial lawyer, was not particularly skilful as a draftsman, nor very profound on the law of real property, and he had no other pupil than me, which, though in many respects of advantage, was, on the whole, I think, rather the reverse. None know the difficulties of a path but those who are treading or have just trodden it.   Difficulties are continually arising; by discussion amongst themselves pupils learn more from each other than from a master.

It is usual for law students to pass one year in the chambers of a conveyancer, and two, or at most three, with a Chancery barrister or a special pleader, according as their destination is to the Common Law or Equity courts.   At a time earlier than mine it had been not uncommon for young men, before they were called, to draw pleadings in Equity, as still is the practice at the Common Law Bar, and to draw them for barristers who had more business than they could manage.   My uncle wished me to adopt this course; and I drew a good deal for him in this way after I had been three years in his chambers, and I think two bills, one for Wingfield, and one for Winthrop, besides a very few pleadings for solicitors.   The pay was most miserable; but the practice was of some value as an introduction to business. It was, however, but shabby work. The practice had then fallen into desuetude, and probably I was the last who adopted it.

In 1815 Mr. Cooke obtained a silk gown, and it would have been of great importance to me to have been called to the Bar at that time, as many of his clients were acquainted with me, and would probably have transferred to me the business which his promotion threw open. By some accident, however, my entry at Lincoln's Inn had been delayed longer than it should have been. Five years of probation were at that time necessary for any one who had not taken a degree at the University; and I was doomed to pass another long year before I could attain the honour of mounting a wig.

It is common, I believe, to consider youth and boyhood as the season of en-

joyment, and cares and sorrows as com-
mencing or increasing with manhood.
With me it was quite otherwise: all my
earliest years were gloomy and joyless, and
I cannot remember one, hardly indeed a
month in the course of them, which I
would willingly live again, whereas there
is hardly one year (if indeed there be
one) since my twenty-fourth which I
would not gladly repeat.   It is well for
philosophers to despise wealth, and preach
up the happiness of virtuous poverty, but
all depends on what is meant by poverty.
That which prevents a man from associating on terms of equality with those who
in birth and station are his equals, especially if female relations are involved in
the humiliations which are the inseparable attendants on the " res angusta domi,"
is a real and substantial evil, and incon-
sistent, unless in minds more happily
tempered than mine, with enjoyment.
The greatest perhaps of satirists has with

perfect truth pointed out its worst ingre-
dient :—

> " Nil habet infelix paupertas durius in se
> Quam quod ridiculos homines facit ;"

and in those days there was much more
reason than there is now for Sydney
Smith's observation, that "in England
poverty is infamous."

No doubt, however, it is to this period,
however little agreeable in itself, that I am
indebted for much of my subsequent success. It was the severe preparation for the
subsequent harvest. I learned to consider
indefatigable labour as the indispensable
condition of success ; pecuniary independence as essential alike to virtue and to happiness; and no sacrifices too great to
avoid the misery of debt. In the whole
course of my life I have never borrowed a
farthing, and I contrived even to make
some small savings out of the pittance of
£100 or £150 a year which I earned
by practising under the Bar.

The period for which I had long panted
arrived at last, and in November, 1816,
I was called to the Bar in a batch of men
which included Purton Cooper and Teed.
Nobody probably ever began a profession
with greater advantages. Almost all my
family had been more or less connected
with the law, and my brother had been received into one of the best solicitors' offices
in London, that of Messrs. Jones and
Green. My long servitude had secured
me against the dangers of what Lord Coke
calls " præpropera praxis et præpostera
lectio," and it is not therefore very sur-
prising that I started into business with
very unusual rapidity. In the first year I
made £600, a thing I believe unheard of
at that time at the Chancery Bar, and each
succeeding year my receipts were larger.
Pupils flocked to me, of whom I had reason
to be proud. My first was George Sanders,
a son of one of the most eminent convey-
ancers at that time; and my second, Plumer,

a son of the Master of the Rolls. Hayter, now Secretary to the Treasury, and Ford, the celebrated author of the ' Handbook of Spain,' were soon added to the list, and Philip Abbott, a son of Lord Colchester, and Elmsley, who has ever since remained the most intimate and valued of my friends. Before I was thirty I was making a professional income of £3000 a year.

The time at which my call to the Bar took place was a very favourable one for young Chancery barristers. Lord Eldon, who had held the Great Seal with but a short interval from the beginning of the century, had for many years obstinately refused to make any new King's Counsel in the court. But in 1815 he made a batch, of whom Mr. Cooke was one, most of whom were too old to profit by the advancement ; and in 1818 he made another batch of younger men, including Horne, Heald, and Wingfield, who had very great practice, and of course by their

removal left a larger spoil to be divided
amongst the juniors. One of the accidents
which probably happen to all men who
prosper in a profession happened to me at
this time and materially improved my position.

Amongst the clients of Mr. Horne was
a firm of Horne and Rogers, who had
one of the most extensive businesses in
London as agents for country solicitors.
Horne was one of the six clerks, and a
brother of the barrister ; and on the promotion of the latter within the Bar the
business of the firm was taken to Temple,
who had been a pupil of Horne's, and his
future was supposed to be made. Within
a few months, however, on going one day
to chambers I was surprised to see some
papers, with the well-known name of
Horne and Rogers on the back, contain-
ing instructions for an answer, and accom-
panied by a note stating that, in consequence of the delay of the counsel be-

.fore whom the papers had been previously laid, the defendant's time for answering had expired, and an attachment had issued. On looking into the matter, I hit upon some trumpery technicality which had been overlooked, by means of which we set aside the attachment and obtained abundant time for answering. From that time till I gave up drawing pleadings, nearly ten years afterwards, Horne and Rogers were constant clients. My chambers were, I think, never without papers from their office, and they paid me in fees on an average above £500 a year.

They were also the means of bringing me into notice in another way. They were employed in 1819 in an election petition by a Captain Thomson, to unseat Sir M. M. Lopes, for bribery at Barnstaple. The case was a very clear one, and the bribery was so gross that the Whigs thought it expedient to take steps for disfranchising the borough, and with that

c

view they brought a bill into the House
of Lords to indemnify against penalties all
the witnesses who might disclose their own
iniquity.   Warren, then in the first practice as a parliamentary counsel, had been
the leader before the committee of the
House of Commons, and he, together with
Cross, a young man at the Common Law
Bar, and myself, were counsel for the Bill
in the House of Lords.   Just, however, at
the moment when we were to attend the
House, we were told that Warren could not
be present.   He had ratted, being a strong
Whig, and accepted the chief-justiceship
of Chester, then usually called the Rat-
trap, and had gone down to be elected
for some borough.   Cross and I were left
to do the best we could, he having very
little experience in such matters, and I
none at all.   The witnesses, who had
spoken with the utmost readiness before
the committee of the House of Commons
when the object was to unseat a member

and have a new election, took quite a different view of the question when the purpose was to disfranchise the borough, and put a stop to their gains in future; and it was with the utmost difficulty that any truth could be extracted from them. However, it was something to be placed in so prominent a position,—to be brought into communication with the great men who supported the Bill; Lord Grey, Lord Holland, Lord Lansdowne, and others; and I remember attending a consultation at Lansdowne House, the only time that I have ever been within its walls. The Chancellor was very civil to the counsel for the Bill; the more so, perhaps, because he was opposed to the measure, and we could make but very little way in establishing our case. I remember he sent down a note to the Bar in these terms:—

" Pemberton had better examine Cross, and Cross Pemberton; they will prove as much as their witnesses."

I believe after this I might have got into practice as a parliamentary counsel, but it would have interfered too much with my business in Chancery to make it desirable. The same reason prevented my going the circuit. It was formerly the custom for Chancery barristers to do so. Lord Eldon, I believe, had a lead on the Northern Circuit, and both Mr. Perceval and Sir Samuel Romilly went the Midland. When a man was made Attorney- or Solicitor-General he gave it up; and, if he was previously at the Common Law Bar, usually took his seat as a barrister in the Court of Chancery. Under these circumstances, the Attorney-General had a fair claim to any office in the court, either that of Master of the Rolls or Chancellor; and the best men at the Bar were qualified for the highest station in either branch of the profession, having usually had experience in both. This was the case with Lord Hardwicke, Lord

Mansfield, and Lord Eldon. But unfortunately the claim to these great offices
has been supposed to remain, when the
qualifications for them have ceased. Lord
Erskine, Lord Lyndhurst, Lord Brougham,
and Lord Campbell, all undertook the
highest judicial office in Chancery, without ever having had the slightest practice
there; and (it may be said without dis-
paragement of their transcendent abilities)
without any knowledge of the science on
their exposition of which millions of property were to depend. It is known, indeed, that Lord Erskine did all he could
to avoid a position for which he was no-
toriously unfit, and endeavoured to induce Lord Ellenborough to take the
Great Seal. I happened myself to be present when gossiping with Sir J. Scarlett,
and some other members of the Bar, at
Howard's coffee-house, after mentioning
a great many anecdotes of his professional
career, he made use of the remarkable ex-

pression, "the most discreditable passage in
my life was sitting in the Court of Chancery." I have heard Lord Brougham
speak in the same sense; indeed, he told
me that when the Government was formed
in 1830, he positively refused to accept
the seals, and only consented to do so when
he was told by Lord Grey that either he
must take them or the attempt to form a
Whig Government must be given up. I
should mention, as one instance of the
great difficulty of ascertaining the truth
about anything, that on mentioning this
conversation to Lord Langdale, he positively asserted that it was inaccurate; he
said, " I know that when Brougham hesitated Lord Grey told him, 'you must
make up your mind at once, if you refuse
I have got my Chancellor ready.'" Lord
Langdale did not say so, but I collected
that he meant that he was the intended
substitute, being at that time in immense
repute amongst Whigs and Radicals both
as a lawyer and as a politician.

When one considers the various duties which belong to the office of Chancellor, it is impossible not to be reminded of the remark of Rasselas to Imlac, who was enumerating the necessary qualifications of a poet. " Enough! Enough!" said the prince, " thou hast said enough to convince me that no man can ever be a poet." Even in the mere judicial business which belongs to the office, few men have possessed the requisite knowledge in more than one branch, if in any. The Scotch Law, for instance, is finally settled in the House of Lords, and it may be safely asserted that neither Lord Lyndhurst, Lord Cottenham, Lord Truro, nor Lord Cranworth ever had any practice in Scotch Law till they were called upon to pronounce upon it in the last resort.

" Revenons à nos moutons." In the Summer circuit of 1817 I joined the Northern circuit at Lancaster, where there was a Court of Chancery in addition to the ordinary court, and there I earned, but was not paid, the sum of half-a-guinea. I was present at the usual saturnalia, where, however, there was less fun and more seriousness than I fancy is usual on such occasions. The present Chief Baron Pollock was tried for what was treated by all as a really grave offence, having dined with an attorney during the circuit. I was not tempted by my success at Lancaster to interrupt my progress in London by going there a second time, and I have often felt my deficiency in the knowledge of Common Law, and especially of the practice of the courts, and what old Littleton calls "la plus honorable et profitable chose, la science de bien plaider."

About this time, for the first and last time in my life, I asked a favour for my own benefit; that is, I applied to the Chancellor for a commissionership of bankruptcy. I had no right to expect it, and received no answer to my letter.

When I was called to the Bar, Sir William Grant was Master of the Rolls, and Lord Eldon Chancellor. Up to 1814 they had done the whole judicial business of the Court of Chancery; Lord Eldon, in addition, presiding of course in the House of Lords, and Sir William Grant usually performing the same duty in the Privy Council. The business of the Court of Chancery fell into arrear, and there was no small outcry against Lord Eldon, when he proposed to have the assistance of a Vice-Chancellor; the spirit of faction, represented, I am sorry to say, by no less men than Brougham and Romilly, attributing the arrears entirely to the fault of Lord Eldon. At the present moment the judicial establishment of the Court of Chancery consists of the Chancellor, the Master of the Rolls, two Lords Justices, and three Vice-Chancellors, and the business of the Privy Council is disposed of by the judicial committee, at which the Master of the Rolls rarely attends.

The establishment of a Vice-Chancellor's office was, unfortunately, not put upon a footing which qualified it for relieving the Chancellor, nor was the choice of the individuals who first held the office in all respects happy. Sir T. Plumer, who was the first Vice-Chancellor, though a most able, laborious, and conscientious man, had learned Equity only on the Equity side of the Exchequer, and did not possess the proper authority over such men as Romilly and Leach, and others, who had spent their lives in the Court of Chancery; and he was very slow. When in 1818 he was succeeded by Leach, a total change took place, but one by no means tending to the relief of the Chancellor.

Sir John Leach was a man of many great qualities, utterly fearless, both morally and physically, of singular clearness of understanding, and a quickness in collecting the facts of a case, and a neatness and precision in the statement of them rarely excelled, of remarkable powers of elocution, of a considerable acquaintance with the technical principles of Equity, and a scorn of everything mean or base. He was outstripping other competitors, and fast advancing to a lead with Sir Samuel Romilly, when he took his seat on the bench. But he had defects as a judge which, perhaps, overbalanced his good qualities. A temper at once irritable and violent, an overweening opinion of his own knowledge, an impatience of all contradiction, and a total want of that calm attention to the arguments of counsel which is absolutely essential to enable a judge either to satisfy suitors or to do justice. I never felt the full force, till I sat myself at the Judicial Committee, of an observation made many years ago by my old friend Sir William Alexander. "Nobody knows how much energy it requires in a judge to hold his tongue."

This was an energy which Leach certainly did not possess, and probably would have despised. When he was first Vice-Chancellor, his interruptions were incessant. As soon as he understood, or fancied he understood the facts, he would hardly listen to argument. He trusted to his knowledge of the principles of equity, and imagined that any decided case which did not square with his notions must be bad law. He came on the Bench with a full determination to clear off the arrears of his Court, which in two or three years he effected ; but he accomplished it by never hearing a case through ; by deciding against the plaintiff on the opening, or against the defendant without hearing a reply ; and there was equal truth and wit in a remark of Rose, in answer to somebody who was speculating on what the Vice-Chancellor would do when he had got through all the causes in his Court. " Do ! why, he will hear the other side."

The contrast of Lord Eldon's slowness made his rapidity more celebrated, and his fame in that respect penetrated where it could hardly have been expected to reach. I remember seeing a coach between Preston and Blackpool, which, to denote its speed, was called " the Vice-Chancellor."

The effect of these proceedings on the part of the Judge was to lead to constant altercations between him and the Bar, which proceeded to such an extent that at one time he had determined to commit Sir E. Sugden, who, with much the same temper and courage, had a wonderful knowledge of cases, which Leach esteemed very lightly. He called into his room some of the leading counsel— I believe all the Queen's Counsel—to speak to them on the subject; but they all dissuaded him from so violent a step, and, I believe, told him that his own violence was the cause of the unpleasant scenes which occurred. No judge that ever existed could have disposed of the same quantity of business in the same time without innumerable mistakes. The offensive manner in which he acted exasperated the counsel, and often occasioned appeals when otherwise they would not have been brought, and the result was that Lord Eldon was more overpowered than ever, and his dilatoriness was more exposed to remark ; for the whole of his time was occupied in rehearing matters which had already been before the Vice-Chancellor ; the business was as much in arrear as ever in his Court, and the suitor was subjected in all doubtful cases to the expense and delay of two hearings, instead of having its merits disposed of by one hearing before Lord Eldon. The old Chancellor was naturally nettled and vexed, and could not always restrain the expression of his feelings. Every word that could anger Leach was of course carefully repeated to him, often probably with additions, by the counsel whom he had offended; and the Vice-Chancellor was on no better terms with his chief than with the Bar.

Lord Eldon was as opposite to Sir John Leach as it was possible for one judge to be to another. Affable alike to seniors and juniors, patient of argument, though seldom in reality paying much attention to it, in knowledge of law of unapproachable superiority to all the men of his day, not only in one branch but in all, in Scotch as well as English, with powers of mind which enabled him thoroughly to grasp and comprehend every legal question that came before him in all its bearings,—he might, but for one unhappy failing, which grew upon him with years, have probably been equal to the greatest Chancellor that ever sat in England. But all his great qualities were marred by irresolution and caution amounting even to timidity. It was justly said of him that

his almost only fault was a distrust of his
own opinion, which nobody else shared.
At the close of a case he would make observations upon it, showing that he was
perfectly master both of the facts and the
law ; would intimate his opinion, which he
perhaps never changed ; and when every-
body was satisfied by his reasoning, instead
of deciding, would take the papers home
with him, for the purpose of further consideration, promising his final judgment
on an early day.   But that day too often
never arrived. Other matters pressed upon
his attention, the case was forgotten, and
the papers were sometimes lost, and after
the lapse of months, and perhaps in some
cases even of years, judgment was obtained
from him with difficulty, or, as occasionally happened, the parties died, or settled
their dispute in utter despair of ever pro-
curing a decision.   It was amusing to
hear him, even when he did give a decision in a case of any difficulty or im-

portance, speaking diffidently of his own judgment, and expressing, apparently with heartfelt sincerity, the consolation which he had in the reflection that there was a superior tribunal by which his views might be corrected,—that superior tribunal consisting of himself, sitting in the House of Lords, with two lay peers probably to assist him.

This infirmity of a great judge was made the more remarkable and more provoking by the vigour which he showed in cases which from their nature admitted of no delay, and which were either not subject to appeal, as in bankruptcy, or in fact never were appealed, as in lunacy. These cases came on by petition, which he had an opportunity of reading before they were heard. On these occasions his dispatch was wonderful, equal to that of the Vice-Chancellor, with the difference that he always thoroughly understood the case in which he made the order, which could

D

not by any means always be asserted of
his deputy. I have seen him myself repeatedly, at the close of the sittings, before
the long vacation, when Parliament was
prorogued, and his mind was not distracted
with politics, begin a long list of lunatic and
bankruptcy petitions,—come into Court
by nine o'clock, sit till four, return at half-
past five, and sit till nine or ten, disposing
of petitions (which he had always read),
and throwing them down to the Registrar
with an Order upon them almost as rapidly as they were called on. On one
petition, " Take your Order"; on another,
" Is there an affidavit of such or such a
fact ?" on a third, "Can you ask for more
than such or such relief ?" On a fourth,
" Is it possible to get over such an objection ? " and, on the other hand, when a
point of legal difficulty arose (and in none
are the difficulties greater than in bankruptcy), he would dispose of the case at
the close of the argument, explaining the

principles of law with the distinctions be-
longing to them, applying them with un-
erring accuracy to the facts of the case,
and exhibiting a familiarity with all the
authorities, usually much greater than that
of the counsel who had studied them for
the purpose of the particular case. Mr.
Cooke had a very great and well-merited
reputation and practice as a lawyer in
bankruptcy; he was no friend of Lord
Eldon, who had used him, he thought, ill;
but I have heard him again and again ex-
press his astonishment at the manner in
which the Chancellor discharged this part
of his duties.

Sir Wm. Grant was essentially different
both from Lord Eldon and Sir J. Leach.
He combined all the qualities of a great
judge in a more complete degree than
any man I have ever seen on the Bench.
He had not indeed the unbounded knowledge of all law, at once profound and
exact, which was so marvellous in the

Chancellor; and I have heard, from men well qualified to form an opinion (Mr. Cooke and Mr. Bell), that when he first took his seat as Master of the Rolls, he was rather deficient in his acquaintance with the rules of the English Courts of Equity. He had never enjoyed very great practice in Chancery, and had been principally employed in Scotch Appeals and at the Cockpit. But his great reputation had been earned in the House of Commons, where he had mingled with Pitt and Fox in the War of Giants. The judicial duties of the Master of the Rolls at that time were not very onerous. He had abundant time to make himself fully master of both the law and the facts of every case which came before him: and when I heard him, long experience had entirely supplied any deficiency which might at any time have existed. He seemed to have been born for a Judge. During the course of an argument he sat on the bench as

immovable and impassive, and almost as
silent, as a statue. He never interrupted
counsel except to ask a question, and that
but very rarely. He never was occupied
with anything but the matter before him,
never reading or writing notes as was too
often the practice on the bench. He appeared to listen with uninterrupted attention to what was said, whoever might say
it. He never indicated by words, or ges-
ture, or even look, till a case was over,
what was the inclination of his opinion.
At the conclusion of the argument usually,
but always after a short interval, he gave
his judgment, and never I think was the
application of pure logic, without the pe
dantry of forms, to the affairs of men so
beautifully exemplified. The discussion
of the evidence, the statement of the facts,
the enunciation of the rules of law by
which the decision was to be governed,
were all faultless; and the conclusion was
an inevitable consequence from the pre-

misses. Nor were the language and manner inferior to the matter. Sir John Leach seemed never to be fully in possession of his powers till he had worked himself into a passion, however little the case might be calculated to interest the feelings. Lord Eldon qualified his propositions with so many restrictions and provisions, and encumbered his sentences with so many parentheses, that it required some pains and attention to extract the ore from the mine in which it was imbedded. But Grant's language was worthy to be the vehicle of the reasoning which it conveyed; pure, clear, unambitious, with no ornament but the exquisite adaptation of the words to the meaning, his style was a model of judicial eloquence. His judgments were delivered in a tone of calmness and dignity, which convinced even those against whom he decided that feeling had no part in the determination; and a fine voice and countenance added grace to a performance calculated to fill all who may occupy a similar position with envy and despair. His demeanour towards the Bar was perhaps a little distant, but perfectly urbane; and he retired from public life in the full possession apparently of all his faculties (though I believe he had suffered from a fit of some kind which he regarded as a warning), amid more sincere and general esteem and regret amongst those whom he left than I have ever seen equalled. He died in the year 1832, the same year which saw the departure from amongst us of two other great men, Sir Walter Scott and Sir J. Mackintosh,—and such was the excitement at that time on the subject of the Reform Bill, that they all passed away with as little observation as if their names had been unknown in England.

Soon after I was called to the bar, that is, in May, 1817, Garrow, the most ignorant man probably that ever held the office of Attorney-General (though very powerful as a speaker to juries, and without a rival as an examiner of witnesses), was made a Baron of the Exchequer. Shepherd, the Solicitor-General, a gentleman, and a good lawyer and an able man (but as deaf as a post), was promoted to be Attorney-General ; and Gifford, then a young man, who had risen rapidly into notice in the common-law courts, and had attracted the notice both of Lord Ellenborough and C. J. Gibbs, was made Solicitor-General. Upon his appointment he took his seat in the Court of Chancery, as had been usual in earlier days, and it was said that he had done so at the instance of Lord Eldon, who, while attacks were continually being made upon him in the House of Commons, insisted on having one of the law officers of the Crown in his court. Gifford was an able man, of great industry, of considerable quickness of apprehension, of remarkable knowledge of those branches of law which he had studied, and of aptitude for acquiring others, as was evinced by his great success in Scotch appeals. But he was not a good speaker, and voice, manner, and elocution were none above the average. In the Court of Chancery he was placed in a very unpleasant position. Called upon to contend in matters of which he was necessarily ignorant with men such as Leach and Romilly, naturally his superiors in power, and who had passed their lives in the practice of the court, he had to fight against fearful odds; and while he was treated by the seniors with little respect, he was regarded with great jealousy by the men who were in the second rank, and were shortly to be moved into the first—by Horne, and Heald, Wingfield, Shadwell, and Sugden, who regarded him as an interloper, and as having been raised over their heads to an office for which each of them probably thought himself to be better qualified. He must have had a very unpleasant time of it in the Court of Chancery, where he never had much business except that which was official. I had no acquaintance with him at all; but he noticed me soon after he began to practise in Chancery, trusted me occasionally with briefs (probably of no great importance) when he was called away; and when, soon afterwards, he was made Attorney-General, and suits were to be instituted by that officer on the report of the Charity Commission, he appointed me to be his deputy, or, in the common phrase, his devil, as to charities, the fees of which must have amounted, I think, on an average to full £300 a year.

At Christmas, 1817, Sir William Grant quitted the bench which he had so highly adorned. I had been employed several times before him, and I remember one instance of his candour and fairness, and anxiety to do justice, which struck me very much at the time, and has ever since dwelt in my memory. In a case of Wood-houselee *v.* Dalrymple, where the question was as to the effect of a gift to an illegitimate child, I held a brief with Sir S. Romilly and Mr. Cooke as counsel for the plaintiff. Sir S. Romilly having opened the case, Sir W. Grant called on the other side, but, in the course of the argument for the defendant, entertained some doubt, said he thought he had been too hasty in stopping the other counsel for the plaintiff, and desired to hear them. Mr. Cooke spoke shortly, as was his wont, and when the defendant's counsel were thereupon about again to proceed, Sir W. Grant interposed, and observed that there appeared to be another gentleman for the plaintiff whom he ought to hear. I accordingly said a few words, the case proceeded, and Sir W. Grant ultimately decided, according to his first impression, for the plaintiff. In the course of a long and extensive experience I cannot call to mind a similar anecdote.

On the retirement of Sir W. Grant, Plumer was made Master of the Rolls, and Leach succeeded him as Vice-Chancellor. Leach had always in Parliament acted with the Whigs, but he had professed himself to be attached to the Prince, and when Adam had been made Chief Commissioner in Scotland, Leach had accepted the office which I now hold of Chancellor of the Duchy of Cornwall, and before he was made Vice-Chancellor had, in fact, ratted. Romilly and he had never been on very good terms. The one was rather supercilious, and the other irritable and impetuous, determined at all cost to succeed, and probably more anxious to provoke, than to avoid, a quarrel with a man at that time at the head of the Bar, but whose superiority he was far from acknowledging. These altercations were very frequent, and on one occasion (before

I was called) Romilly was exasperated into applying the term *impertinent* to something which Leach had said or done. Leach immediately left the Rolls Court, at which this scene took place, and sent a note insisting on an immediate apology or a hostile meeting. Romilly preferred the former alternative. Leach felt his advantage, and used it not very generously. Leach had great power of sarcasm, and a very insulting tone towards his adversaries ; and I have been present myself on more than one occasion when Sir S. Romilly has appealed to the Court against Leach's behaviour. Lord Eldon had a good deal of difficulty in keeping the peace between them. I remember a parting blow which Romilly dealt to his adversary just before his promotion to the Bench. The Habeas Corpus Act was at that time suspended. Leach, in opposing a motion for the new trial of an issue, had insisted much on the right of juries to decide finally, and

Romilly, in his reply, observed that "he listened with pleasure to such sentiments from one whom public rumour had marked out for a high judicial position, that his learned friend no doubt remembered that the Habeas Corpus Act and trial by jury were the two safeguards of liberty, and clung, like a fond mother who had lost one child, with increased affection to the other."

After the change took place in their relative positions, the conduct of these two great rivals to each other was creditable, I think, to both. Romilly treated the Judge with the respect due to his office; and Leach showed to the counsel the attention to which his great station and talents entitled him, and a forbearance not extended to others; at least, though violent altercations between the Bar and the Bench were too common, I do not remember any in which Sir S. Romilly was a party. Unhappily, however, the trial was very short, for in less than a twelvemonth Romilly, overwhelmed with grief for the loss of his wife, died by his own hand.

This sad event happened, I think, on the day when the Court of Chancery was to resume its sittings after the Long Vacation of 1818. Lord Eldon, it was said, burst into tears on seeing the vacant seat which had been so long filled by the great advocate, between whom and himself there never had passed anything but the most dignified courtesy in public, or, as far as I know, in private, notwithstanding the violent opposition of their political views.

When I knew Sir Samuel Romilly his business was so great, and he was so much engaged in politics, that, in spite of his great industry, he was seldom master of his case when he opened it. Having the complete lead of the Court, he was almost always for the plaintiff or the petitioner, and had therefore to begin. I have often seen his briefs with a short abstract of the

facts and dates on the back of the first
sheet, which had been made by some one
who had read the brief for him (usually, I
believe, his nephew), and from this, and
what he had picked up at consultation, he
was accustomed to state his case ; his opening, therefore, was often loose, sometimes
purposely so, in order to allow greater
scope for the reply. This course, very
convenient for a counsel, but not very fair
towards his opponents, was encouraged by
the habits of Lord Eldon, who always
heard a case from the beginning to the
end, though his opinion was probably
made up as soon as he had collected the
facts, and who used to justify the practice
by saying, half in jest and half in earnest,
that when the defendants had failed in sa-
tisfying him that the plaintiff was wrong,
the plaintiff's counsel often succeeded in
doing so in his reply.

As an advocate I think Sir Samuel Romilly approached in his own line as near

perfection as it is possible for man to attain. He was familiar with the law and the practice of the court himself, and was aware that they were equally well known to the judges whom he addressed; he did not, therefore, waste time in arguing points which were untenable; he transacted the ordinary run of business like a man of business, without aiming at anything more, *par negotiis neque supra.* But when any great occasion arose, especially when he came to reply at the close of a long and important case, in which the feelings were at all engaged, nothing could be finer. Usually restating his case (which of course his opponents had misunderstood), not always exactly as he had opened it, but as, after the discussion which it had undergone, it could be presented with the best prospect of success; noticing all the arguments which had been used against him, and which admitted of an answer, with as much fairness as it is usual with counsel (which

E

perhaps is not saying much); clear, powerful, and logical when he was right, discreet
and adroit when he was wrong ; never in-
troducing an unnecessary sentence, seldom
using a word that could be altered for the
better ; always energetic, often earnest and
impassioned, never degenerating into violence, either of language or tone ; with a
noble countenance, a stately figure, or
what seemed such when drawn up to its
height and clothed in his robes, and a
voice distinct, deep, and mellow, always,
as it seemed to me, modulated with singular skill,—the exhibition was one which
it was impossible to witness without admiration and delight.   Probably they who
have heard Sir William Grant and Sir
Samuel Romilly have heard the most exquisite specimens of eloquence ever addressed from the Bar to the Bench, or
from the Bench to the Bar.   Oratory to
juries and to popular assemblies is of course
quite a different matter.   Whether, if Sir

Samuel Romilly had lived to attain the Chancellorship, he would have been as great as a judge as he was at the Bar must be considered as doubtful, having regard to the very rare instances in which the same men have been equally eminent in both characters. He seemed to possess all the requisites, but he might have been found deficient in the temper and patience which, though the least showy, are not the least important qualities of a judge. "Omnium consensu capax imperii, nisi imperasset," is a maxim of too frequent application to all great stations.

With all Sir Samuel Romilly's great merits, he was not, I think, very popular at the Bar. He took no pains to make himself agreeable; his manners were a little severe, and, at all events, he had not the reckless gaiety and familiar cordiality which made Erskine and Brougham and Copley the idols of their juniors in the same profession.

The removal from the Bar of Leach and of Romilly, and of Richards, who had been made Chief Baron of the Exchequer, left a clear course for the new King's Counsel of 1818. Of those who had been made in 1815, only one had established any great position, viz. Mr. Bell, who after Sir J. Leach's appointment confined himself to the Vice-Chancellor's Court. His success was achieved against disadvantages which would have seemed to be insurmountable in a profession where any kind of oratory was required. His voice was thick and inharmonious, his utterance indistinct, his sentences perplexed and confused and never completed, his figure awkward and deformed, with a club-foot, a head with fiery red hair, a huge mouth, and features altogether as plain as could be consistent with a uniform expression of benevolence and good-humour. His handwriting was totally illegible to all who were not by long habit familiar with it;

and when it was deciphered the opinions which were expressed in it were almost as difficult to be understood as the hieroglyphics in which their meaning was enshrouded. Against all these obstacles the unconquerable energy of the man prevailed. The confusion of his expression did not reach his mind. He had obtained high distinction—I believe had been a Senior Wrangler—at Cambridge. His powers of application were extraordinary, and exerted to the uttermost; his knowledge of law inferior only to Lord Eldon's; his knowledge of the practice of the Court, and all the intricacies of pleading, probably superior. His quickness in detecting an objection of this kind in his adversary's case, and his ingenuity in meeting one when raised to his own, were unsurpassed. He always thoroughly knew his brief, even before the consultation, at which, instead of picking up the facts from his junior and hearing his view, he explained his own.

In speaking before Leach, no provocation, either from the Bench or the Bar, ever disturbed him. He yielded for the moment, but always returned again to the charge, and persisted till he found the Court was fully in possession of his argument. Nor when the victory was won against him, and the battle seemed to be over, did his efforts cease : on the contrary, he often deprived the conqueror of the spoil. He had an unrivalled knowledge, amongst other matters of form, of the forms of orders and decrees, which he had copied from time to time in the course of his practice. The directions to be given and the inquiries to be made in Chancery are often of extreme difficulty and complication, and it often is necessary to recur to the Court to settle the minutes. On those occasions Bell's astuteness was without parallel. Few of the counsel knew anything of the forms, or cared to engage in the tiresome details ; Bell would not unfrequently, when a hasty decision had been pronounced at the hearing, get it really reversed under pretence of settling the proper language of the order. Or if the judgment was not altered, he would introduce some declaration in his client's favour, or qualify some which was against him, or suggest some accounts and inquiries seemingly very innocent, but by means of which, when the cause came on again, it not unfrequently appeared that the matter was really left open. So great was his success that he obtained the lead in the Court very shortly after he entered it, and maintained it unimpaired as long as he remained in it. So highly was his opinion valued, notwithstanding the strange mode in which it was usually written and expressed, that he was continually obliged to refuse cases, even when parties would be content to wait for months in order to obtain it.

He excelled all his competitors at the

Bar, and indeed all the men whom I have ever known, in kindliness of disposition and readiness to impart information. When a man is deeply engaged in his own business, worried perhaps and wearied, there are few things more annoying than being interrupted by the questions of others, especially of those who have no claim upon you. Yet to Bell, when in the fullest practice, I have repeatedly gone when I was very young at the Bar, to consult him on some difficulty which had occurred, and have always been treated with the same kindness and consideration. He would not only give the information if he had it in his head, but would take down his books or refer to his precedents, and seem rather pleased to be able to give assistance than vexed at being asked for it. What happened to me happened in like manner to all others who applied to him; his good nature was inexhaustible. Though sometimes a little joked for his peculiarities, his sterling qualities procured him universal respect, and he was certainly more beloved than any man in the profession.

5th June, 1857.

My progress at the Bar was uninterrupted, and I was rash enough to diminish my business by giving up successively the attendance on commissions of bankruptcy, of which I think I attended but one ; on commissions of lunacy, which I never attended at all, though invited to do so ; and the Court of Exchequer, where I had a good deal of practice. And ultimately I took a most dangerous step, and which might have proved a fatal one if I had not soon afterwards obtained a silk gown. I gave up drawing altogether, and of course my pupils with it, trusting to the pleadings which I had already drawn, and to some little leading business which I had acquired, to keep me afloat till I got within the Bar.

In 1823 a circumstance occurred which brought me in some degree into notice. Rothschild was defendant in a suit by a person named Doloret, who had filed a bill for the specific performance of a contract with respect to a share in a foreign loan. Under the advice of Bell and myself, he had demurred to the bill on the ground that from the nature of the transaction time was of the essence of the contract, and that the delay of a day might totally change the nature of the risk. The case was new and of vast importance to the defendant, who indeed could not possibly have carried on his business if the plaintiff had succeeded. Briefs were delivered to Bell and to me to support the demurrer against Sugden and some junior, who were counsel for the plaintiff; but when the cause was in the paper for argument Bell had retired from court business, and confined himself to chamber practice, and could not be prevailed upon to argue the case. I was therefore left alone to argue it, and succeeded. The case is reported in 1 Simon and Stuart, p. 590. Rothschild was very much pleased, and made me a present of a gold snuff-box, and when afterwards, in the year 1825, the British and Foreign Alliance Insurance Company came out under his auspices, at a high premium, he allotted to me fifty shares, the highest number allowed to anybody, by which I made £750, the only speculation in which I ever engaged.

17th August, 1859.

I am sorry to see that more than two years have passed since I wrote the above notes, and I have little excuse to offer to myself for their abandonment during so long a period. Indolence I am afraid has been the main cause, at least for the greater part of the time; since last November I have been abundantly occupied with public business.

Up to the year 1825 I was accustomed to spend all my vacations abroad, and by these means I contrived to see a good deal of Europe, or at least what was considered a good deal for a lawyer in those days, when vacations were shorter than they are now, and neither railroads nor even steamboats were invented. I contrived to visit many of the principal cities in Europe,—Paris, Berlin, Dresden, Prague, Vienna, Trieste, Venice, Milan, Rome, and Madrid; the latter place I went to in 1821 with Hayter, now Sir W. G. Hayter, who had lately been my pupil. In 1825 I went across the water for the last time for many years with Mr. and Mrs. Radcliffe and their two daughters, then two of the finest women in England.

I do not know that anything noteworthy happened in my professional life till I got a silk gown, except a failure, which if my position had been less strong might have had serious consequences. It may be worth mentioning as an instance of the scandalous manner in which justice was then administered in the House of Lords.

A man of the name of Brookman had long gambled in the French funds, employing Rothschild as his agent, who executed his orders, supplying *Rentes* from time to time out of his own stock, at the market price of the day. After this had gone on for a considerable time, Brookman had lost a large sum of money by his speculations, to the amount of near £20,000; and he bethought himself of the expedient of applying to this transaction the rule relating to principal and agent, by which all sales by the agent to the principal may be set aside, and the agent must account for any loss, but can derive no profit. Sugden was retained by the plaintiff, and Chatfield, who was Rothschild's attorney, determined not to employ any King's Counsel, but to trust the defence entirely to Knight Bruce and myself, who were then both without the Bar. This was of course a marked distinction for two junior barristers, but the result was, as regarded the defendant, very disastrous. Shadwell, who was much under the control of Sugden, made a violent decree in his favour, and the Jew not only had a very large sum to pay, but was heartily abused by the leading counsel against him, and the abuse in a considerable degree sanctioned by the judge.

As the decree was, I believe, utterly wrong, and the case excited a good deal of attention, Rothschild was furious; and probably both he and the public attributed the mischief in a great degree to the inefficiency of his advocates, which to two young gentlemen then struggling for admission within the Bar was no slight discouragement.

The case was afterwards heard upon appeal in 1832, when Brougham was Chancellor, during the heat of the Reform Bill, and just at the time when a great debate on the subject was to come on in the Lords. Knight Bruce was leading counsel with me for the appeal, having then our silk gowns. Brougham was engaged in preparing his speech for the Reform Bill. After evincing the most scandalous partiality, in extending to Sugden, of whom he was in great terror, an indulgence which he refused to us, he sat for some time on the case without even the semblance of attention. In the course of the argument, which lasted for two or three days, he sent for Lord Wynford to assist him, who knew no more of Equity than he did himself. At the close of the argument Lord Wynford got up, and, holding the papers, which were very voluminous, in his hand, he said that of course it could not be supposed that he had read through such a mass, and that he had not heard the whole of the argument, but that he had heard quite enough to convince him that the appeal ought to be dismissed with costs ; and dismissed it was, neither of the judges who sat having the least knowledge of a case admitted to be of the first impression, and of which even if the principle were right (which I am satisfied myself that it is not) was carried out in details which nobody could attempt to justify.

I have known in the course of a long life many cases in which gross injustice has been done; but anything so utterly shameless as the proceedings in the House of Lords in the case of Brookman *v*. Rothschild I never yet witnessed ; and I think a repetition of such a scene is now impossible. It was a case which would have well justified the impeachment of both the learned lords, yet such was the excitement at the time about the Reform Bill,

and such the unbounded popularity of the
Chancellor, that any job, however outrageous, might be perpetrated by a Minister
not only with impunity, but amid accla-
mations of those who imputed every attack
on an officer of the Government to a
desire to stop the Reform Bill.

In 1823, on the retirement of Dallas,
Gifford was made Chief Justice of the
Common Pleas, with a peerage. I was
his *Colt*, that is to say, carried about the
rings which he distributed on being made
a Serjeant; and he continued to treat me,
as he had always done, with great kindness.
It was a curious circumstance that the
first day he sat at Nisi Prius he tried an
action brought by a courier, of the name
of Pupel, against me for wages. I had
refused to give him a character, for he had
imposed upon me with respect to his
knowledge of German at Trieste, where I
had engaged him; but I gave him a certificate that he had travelled with me from

F

that city; and, unfortunately, in paying him, on arriving in this country, I omitted to take a receipt from him. I proved, however, the fact of payment by my cousin Richard, who was present, and the expression by the man of his gratitude when we parted. However, Serjeant Vaughan, who was for the plaintiff, made a rattling speech against me; asked what a man deserved for having his bones shaken all the way from Trieste to London; said that when he would have been glad to see a little of my ready rhino I had given him a certificate under my broad seal, etc. etc.; and, though of course the judge summed up strongly against the plaintiff, the jury found a verdict against me. Both Lord Gifford and the Serjeant laughed with me afterwards, and inquired why I had not moved for a new trial. My answer was that I must at all events have paid the costs of the first, and, as the damages were only £20, I thought it better to submit. This is my only experience of the merits of that Palladium ·of English liberties, Trial by Jury.

In 1824 Lord Gifford was transferred to the Rolls, on the death of Sir Thomas Plumer, and remained there till the autumn of 1826, when by his death I lost a very kind friend. I remember hearing of his death at Whitley, where I was staying with my mother for a day or two, with Miss Leigh, on my road into Lancashire, little thinking at that time that I should ever become the owner of the property of which it forms a part. Gifford was succeeded at the Rolls by Copley, the Attorney-General, who remained at the Rolls till the spring of the following year, when, on Canning's accession to office, on the illness of Lord Liverpool, he accepted the Great Seal, with the title of Lord Lyndhurst.

The circumstances of his appointment to the office of Chancellor were singular, and characteristic both of himself and of the new Premier. I have often heard him repeat the anecdote with great glee. While he was at the Rolls, one of the great debates on the Catholic question came on. Copley, who was member for Cambridge, made a strong speech against the measure. A clever pamphlet on the subject had been published by Philpotts, now Bishop of Exeter; and this pamphlet Copley having seen, used the arguments contained in it with great success in his speech, but without acknowledging the source from which they were derived. Somebody on the other side found him out, and put the pamphlet into Canning's hands, who used his advantage most unmercifully; and, after quoting passages from the pamphlet, and then reminding the House of the corresponding passages of Copley, concluded, amidst roars of laughter, with the words, "This was Toby Philpot." Philpotts himself happened to be under the gallery at the time, though unknown to Canning, who often expressed his regret at the opportunity which he had lost.

When Canning became Prime Minister, and all the Tories refused to serve with him, he offered the Great Seal to Copley, who at the time was performing his duties as Recorder, I think, of Bristol. On his way home he was met at an inn by a King's messenger with a dispatch from Canning, which, on opening it, he found to contain these words, "Will you be Chancellor, *non obstante Philpotto?*"

Lord Lyndhurst was engaged to dine the following week at a large political party of his old colleagues, I forget at what house, and, having abandoned them to their great annoyance, he had some doubt whether he should keep his engagement. After consulting with his wife, however (the then Lady Lyndhurst), they determined that it would be cowardly to stay away, and that they would face it out. Lord Lyndhurst says that he took down to dinner Mrs. Arbuthnot, who did nothing but reproach and abuse him the whole time that he sat by her; but Lady Lyndhurst was taken down by Lord Eldon, who was most marked in his attentions and courtesy to her, and in enabling her to overcome the awkwardness of the position in which she could not but feel that she was placed.

Soon after Lord Lyndhurst's appointment some new King's Counsel were made, amongst others Brougham and my great friend (as he afterwards became) Bickersteth. These promotions sufficiently showed on what political support Canning relied. Brougham and Sir F. Burdett, Bickersteth's great friend, were his main backers in the House of Commons, and sat, as I have understood, immediately behind him. I have often talked with men who were either in office or connected with those who were in office at that time, and my firm persuasion is that it was neither personal dislike to Canning nor jealousy of his abilities, nor difference from him on political subjects, that induced all the principal Tories to decline serving under him. Indeed, as far as politics go, I imagine that he was willing to adopt any, as indeed he showed by consenting, as a condition of office being conferred upon him, that the Catholic question should not be brought forward. One and all with whom I have spoken on the subject said that he was a man on whom they could place no reliance; that in or out of office he was always intriguing against some with whom he was acting.

His career as Prime Minister was a very short one; he died, I think, in August, 1827, having, according to the declared opinion of the Duke of Wellington, as I have heard, done more mischief to the foreign policy of this country in the few months that he held office than twice as many years would suffice to correct. This is not the place to consider that question. Certainly he totally changed the policy of the country; his assistance to Russia against Turkey, and his establishment of anarchy in South America by the recognition of the independence of the Spanish colonies, when they were quite unfit to govern themselves, which he boastfully termed " calling a new world into existence to redress the balance of the old," do but little credit to his sagacity. His principles have been since followed in this country; and the result is that at the present moment (1859) we have not amongst the Governments, either of the Old or New World, a single cordial ally, while the people in the different kingdoms in whose favour we have declaimed, and used what we call our moral influence, universally regard us as agitators, who excite for our own purposes disturbances and insurrections, and desert in the hour of need those whom we have stimulated to resistance to their governors.

In 1829 I applied to Lord Lyndhurst for a silk gown, and received a very civil answer, in which he said that he quite recognised my claim, and that but for my short standing at the Bar he should have made me on the last occasion; accordingly, soon afterwards, in July, 1829, I was called within the Bar.

At this time the Master of the Rolls had been accustomed to sit only of an evening, three evenings a week during term, and every evening, except Saturdays, out of term, sitting, however, in the morning for a week after each term. · It was determined, however, that the evening sittings should be given up, and Leach agreed to sit of a morning as many hours on the whole as he was accustomed to sit under the old arrangement. This led to a division of the King's Counsel between the Vice-Chancellor's and the Rolls Court. Knight Bruce, who received his silk gown at the same time that I did, chose the

Vice-Chancellor's Court, and Tinney, who was also one of the new batch, and I sat down in the Rolls Court, where Bickersteth had the complete lead. I very soon got the second place in the court; indeed, Bickersteth and I divided the business between us, though he always kept the lead, at least as long as Sir John Leach remained. In stating a case he was admirable, clear, fair, bringing out all his facts in the best manner for his clients; stating all the points of law which arose with the greatest distinctness; while his countenance, voice, manner, and high character gave weight and authority to everything he said. But he was not a *handy* counsel : if any objection was unexpectedly started in the course of an argument, he was not ready with an answer; he was not very quick in seeing or inventing distinctions; and, unless he had time for consideration, he was not powerful in reply. As long as Leach remained these deficiencies were not much observed.

As he was usually for the plaintiff, and always stated his case fully and fairly, Leach made up his mind pretty much upon the opening; if he was against the plaintiff, he decided at once; if he was with him, his opinion was not often changed by the defendant's argument; and, consequently, he scarcely ever heard a reply. When Pepys came to be Master of the Rolls the case was very much altered; he always heard a reply, and during the short time that he remained there I think I was gradually gaining upon Bickersteth, though I do not know that I could ever be said to have passed him.

In 1830 an event happened which has decided the course of my subsequent life. Sir Robert Leigh, who had retired from Parliament in 1820, and had amassed by prudence and frugality a very large property, in addition to his patrimonial estate, though he had been always fond of Mr. and Mrs. Cooke, had kept up no intercourse with the rest of the family, and, indeed, had apparently an aversion to them. The family estates had been settled by his father, in default of issue of his own body, on the issue of his brother (my grandfather), and would have been divided therefore (if the limitation had taken effect) amongst his five daughters, of whom my mother was the eldest. This settlement had greatly annoyed Sir Robert, and indisposed him towards those who had the chance of benefiting by it. In 1828 or 1829 he quarrelled with the Rector of Wigan, who claimed tithes of the Hindley Hall estate, which Sir Robert insisted was covered by a farm modus. The Rector filed a bill in Chancery, and set down his cause at the Rolls. Sir Robert endeavoured to retain Bickersteth, and was very angry when he found that he was retained on the other side. Still greater was Sir Robert's vexation when he was told that I was the next in busi

ness in the court, and that he must engage me. He submitted, however, though
I believe with a very bad grace, said I
was a mere boy, and, in short, considered
his case as sacrificed. When his attorney,
Mr. Gaskell, who was a perfect stranger
to me, came to the consultation, I observed that I believed I had some interest,
or might have some interest, in the estate;
when he informed me that the entail had
been found faulty, and that Sir Robert
had barred the remainder, after the limita-
tions to his own issue and his brother, and
their issue male. This did not much dis-
turb me. On looking into the evidence
I found that there was a fatal blot in
our case. In order to maintain a Farm
Modus it was necessary to state. precisely
what lands were covered by it, and, if any
were improperly included or improperly
omitted, the Modus was held to be ill
laid, and a decree went against the defendant. On looking at an old map of the

estate, I found that a small piece of land, taken in from Pennington Green some fifty years before, was included in our answer as part of the ancient farm; the only chance for us was that the blot might not be hit.

We went into court on the memorable morning of the hearing of the cause— memorable to me from its consequences— with not much confidence; and up to this time I had never seen Sir Robert in the course of the proceedings, though I learned afterwards that he had attended the Rolls Court for several days before in order to judge how far he was likely to be ruined by the inability of his counsel. I fancy that he was a little reassured.

In the course of the argument for the plaintiff, poor Sutton Sharpe, who was with Bickersteth, made an attack on Sir Robert's grandfather, who had been a great attorney at Wigan, to whose artifices he attributed a part of the circumstances which appeared favourable to the defendant. I had therefore the double task of vindicating my ancestor and maintaining the Modus, and succeeded so well that, after the case was over, judgment being reserved, Sir Robert came up and introduced himself to me, loaded me with compliments the most extravagant and absurd, said I had vindicated the name of the family and done everything that could be done for the case, and now he did not care what was the result of it, he was perfectly satisfied. A few days afterwards his joy was complete by a judgment being pronounced in his favour. Though the matter could not have been one of £50 a year in value, he was as deeply interested in it as if it had involved as many thousands. In the following year his brother Roger died, principally in consequence of the violent injuries which he had sustained at the Wigan election. In the autumn of that year I paid Sir Robert a visit for a few days at Hindley, when he received me with the greatest affection, said I was welcome to the hall of my ancestors, and set me at the top of the table, with the important words :—

" *Aggredere, et votis jam nunc adsuesce vocari.*"

Soon afterwards he publicly announced me as his heir, and showed me his will, which he had executed before going to the election at Wigan in June, 1831, when I believe he fully expected to be murdered, and where the event all but justified his apprehension.

It has always seemed to me that my introduction to Sir R. Leigh is one of the most remarkable examples which I have ever seen of the important effects produced by circumstances apparently trivial, and which we are accustomed to call fortuitous. If the cause had come on for hearing some months earlier, or been set down in another court, I should probably have had nothing to do with it. If Bickersteth had not been already retained for the plaintiff, no doubt I should have been his counsel, and should have been obliged, probably, to make the observations which gave so much offence to Sir Robert when made by Sharpe. At all events, I must have contended against his interest, and probably might have defeated him by observing the blot to which I have alluded, and which he would naturally have considered as a mere trick. In any event, the chance is that I should have lost or have failed to gain some £12,000 or £14,000 a year.

In June, 1831, another important event occurred to me : I came into Parliament in the hottest crisis of the Reform Bill. I had been for some time ambitious of this distinction, and Mr. Cooke had always spoken of it as the only sure road to office at the Bar. On the dissolution which

G

took place in consequence of the division on General Gascoyne's motion it was proposed to me to stand for Rye, one of the Cinque Ports. The proposal was made through my old pupil Fane, the brother of the beautiful Mrs. Arbuthnot; and it was suggested to me, as one of the advantages, that such a seat would bring me into connection with the Lord Warden, the Duke of Wellington. I saw Mr. Arbuthnot, and agreed to stand. The terms were that I should stand with Pusey, who had come in at the last election; that I should pay him on being returned (I think) £2400; that I should go down to be elected, the seat being quite safe,—Pusey himself, it was said, being unwilling to leave home, on account of the illness of his wife. Down I went accordingly, with Elmsley as my companion, little expecting either of us the scene which awaited us. We slept on the road, and got to Rye, to the house where our voters were to assemble, between nine and ten o'clock. The whole number of voters was, I think, twenty-seven; about fifteen were assembled to meet me, two or three were ill or absent, and not more than six or seven could possibly be brought against us. But the town was in a ferment. The market-place, which lay between our place of meeting and the Town Hall, where the proceedings were to commence, was full of an infuriated mob. Colonel Evans, now Sir De Lacy Evans, who had attempted to open the borough without success at the last election, and had since been to try his chance in vain at some other place, had just returned, utterly desperate and determined, I have not the least doubt, to carry the election, not only by violence, but if necessary by bloodshed. He addressed the populace in the most furious language, and excited them to such a degree that it was impossible for our party to cross to the Town Hall. As the mayor was with us, and nothing could be done without him, the opposite party sent a message to say that they would guarantee us a safe-conduct to the hustings. One of our number, wiser than the rest, suggested that we should stipulate for a safe conduct *back again*, but this was thought too lawyer-like, and a useless precaution when it was supposed we were dealing with gentlemen. Accordingly we went to the Town Hall, where the nomination was made. I desired to be introduced to my opponent, which he declined; and we then went to the hustings, where the poll was to be taken, which consisted of some butchers' shambles close to the hall. Here the suspicions of our cautious friend were but too well justified. Colonel Evans made a most inflammatory speech; said that it was not to be wondered at if the people were driven to madness and blood was shed; that he had guaranteed our safe-conduct there, but nothing further. Thirty years nearly have since elapsed, and even now, looking back coolly at this man's conduct, I cannot conceive how any extravagance of public opinion or of disappointed ambition could convert a man in the position of an officer and a gentleman into the thorough ruffian, which he appeared at this election. When he had finished I addressed the multitude, and I confess they listened to me better than I could reasonably expect. I was a stranger, not mixed up with the former election, which had been attended with great bitterness, and in which a very strong feeling had been excited against Pusey, as afterwards appeared. I was making, or fancied I was making, some way, when a blackguard of the opposite party pulled from under me the chair on which I was standing, brought me down to the ground, and stopped my harangue.

The voting then commenced, amidst a scene of tumult and abuse and violence towards my voters which was frightful.

But the most frightful of all was an inci-
dent which occurred when a very respec-
table old man went up to tender his vote
for me and Pusey: his son, a Radical,
rushed forward, seized him by the throat,
insisted that he should take the bribery
oath, and called him a perjured old villain,
for that he knew he had received a bribe.
This was a little too strong even for some
of the Colonel's supporters; whether for
the Colonel himself I do not know. The
voters on the opposite side were soon
polled out, but it was so obvious that the
election could not end without outrageous
riots and loss of life, unless some compro-
mise was entered into, that Dr. Lamb, the
patron of the borough, said to me that
he was very sorry, but that he strongly
advised that we should be content with
returning one member; that he did not
think our voters would venture to come
up; that Pusey must of course be his
first care; that his arrangements were with

him, and that he would advise me to retire. I told him, with perfect truth, that,
if I had had the least idea of what was in
store for me, I would never have come
near Rye; but, having come, and being in
the thick of it, I would not retire; that
he knew best what the result was likely to
be; and that if he chose to give up the
contest it would be his act, and I should be
satisfied. " No," he said ; " if I was willing
to run the risk of what might follow, he
would stand by me to the last;" and he
immediately went up to the polling-booth.
When he was seen by the mob the yell
set up by the bloodthirsty ruffians was
appalling; he turned round to them with
an undaunted countenance, and exclaimed
(I shall never forget his words), " Do you
expect to terrify me with your violence?
Let any man look in my face and see if it
changes colour; let him come up and lay
his hand on my heart and feel if it beats
one pulse the quicker. In the name of

God and my country, I vote for Pusey and Pemberton." I believe the populace was awed by his courage, which I never saw equalled in similar circumstances. His risk and mine were quite different. I was a stranger, and might easily escape, and at all events the next day should be at a distance; he was a resident on the spot, with a house close to the town, and known, of course, to all the villains who might wish to wreak their spite upon him.

Immediately afterwards a gang, organized no doubt for the purpose, and said to consist mainly of Batmen, or men along the shore, who run down with bludgeons to assist smugglers in their operations, made a rush upon the hustings, entered the polling-booth, and cleared the place, the object being partly to put a stop to the election, which of course could only legally end in the return of Pusey and myself, and partly to carry off the remaining voters, there being, as was said, a schooner lying off shore, in which they were to be removed. This last part of the story is only hearsay, but it is very likely to be true. When the rush was made, a gentleman, I rather believe of the opposite party, said to me, "You are not known; stand up with me close to this wall, and when the mob has passed I will take you by some back lanes to Dr. Lamb's house." I adopted his advice, and reached the doctor's quarters thoroughly vexed and tired. Elmsley, who was with me, escaped much in the same way. There was a young lieutenant in the Navy, of the name of Francillon, a most violent democrat and partisan of Evans, who had brought us the safe-conduct. Elmsley appealed to him, said that he had trusted to his word, which he of course considered extended to the return as well as to the first transit, and called upon him to redeem his promise. He at once admitted it, and said he would perform it; he took Elmsley under his arm, and we met at our worthy patron's, greatly downcast and discomfited. And our spirits were not cheered by our fare, for the doctor, expecting no guests, had prepared no dinner, though matters had so turned out that he had a considerable number on his hands, who probably thought that, under the circumstances, they were safer out of the town than in it. Truth compels me to say that I never saw a more melancholy party or a worse dinner. After it was over we consulted as to the course to be taken. Fortunately I had brought with me, or at least retained to meet me at Rye, Mr. Heptinstall, of the firm of Howe and Heptinstall, of strong Conservative opinions, and not unused to electioneering matters. By his advice, we determined to send round the country for troops to suppress the riots and enforce order; and the next morning when I woke I found eighty blue-jackets, Preventive Service men, and a certain number of dragoons encamped on the doctor's lawn. But our enemies had not been inactive on their side : they had torn up the pavements, fixed cables across the ends of the streets, and declared their determination to resist to the death, and lay the town in ashes, unless Evans was returned as one of the members. Our voters were frightened, and refused to come to the poll. I felt, with Dr. Lamb, that there was no alternative but to abandon the contest ; and, as I readily admitted that Pusey had the best right to the seat, and I should save my £2400, I ordered horses to my carriage and set off on my return to town, where I arrived about ten or eleven o'clock. I sent over to Pusey to inform him of the result, that he was elected and I was defeated. He came over immediately to condole with me, expressed his deep regret, had no doubt I should easily obtain another seat before long, and so forth, and took his leave. He had hardly left me, before, about twelve o'clock at night, a knock was heard at my door, and in walked Heptinstall, who had stayed behind to settle some accounts. He surprised me with the intelligence that, though the Radicals had agreed to return one and one, they would not hear of Pusey, who had given great offence at the last election, and who they thought ought to have come down instead of sending me; that the doctor had been obliged to give way; and, in short, that I was member for Rye with Colonel Evans. I sent once more to Pusey and returned him his condolences and good wishes; he did not seem to be much surprised, and never showed any dissatisfaction with the result. He came in soon afterwards for some nomination borough in Ireland.

Such was my first entry into the House of Commons. I have always felt that I was to blame in not bringing the circumstances before Parliament. But Pusey had taken the whole management of the busi-

ness before the election, and begged that
the matter might be left to him. I found
that our party had given some handle to
the other side, for, in consequence of the
riots which were expected, Billy Holmes
had sent down White-Headed Bob, and
half a score of bruisers, to make fight for us.
This was found out, as it was sure to be,
and it would not have been difficult to at-
tribute the violence which took place to
the popular indignation at such a pro-
ceeding. A good many heads were broken, and one man was said to have been
killed; but, though much hurt, I believe
he recovered.

I never shall forget the night in which,
after so much excitement, I found myself
a Member of Parliament. I threw myself
upon my knees, and earnestly prayed to
the Source of all strength that I might be
enabled to perform faithfully and success-
fully the duties which belong to that position.

Lawyers are generally supposed not to be very well heard in the House, but neither my recollection of what I have heard nor my experience of what I have seen, extending together to half a century, I think, confirms the common opinion. Sir William Grant, Brougham, and Plunket were amongst the greatest orators and most favourite speakers in the palmiest days of Parliamentary eloquence ; and Follett and Cairns have maintained the same station in later days. Of one ordinary failing of my profession, an eagerness to speak more often than the audience is disposed to listen, I could not be accused. I think nobody ever felt more nervous or more unwilling to open his mouth than I did, although I believe I did not show it much in my manner after I had once begun. My first impression, on taking my seat, and listening for a few evenings to the discussion, was one of total disappointment. I had foolishly supposed that the

speaking there was something quite different from, and infinitely superior to, what I
was accustomed to hear in courts of justice, whereas for above a fortnight I was
in the House every night, heard the great
speakers on both sides in the ordinary dis-
cussions which arose, and thought that
none of them were better, and many of
them not so good, as the lawyers. This,
however, was owing entirely to the want
of a subject worthy to excite eloquence.
The first speech which I heard in the least
degree approaching to that character, and
which at all excited my admiration or envy,
was one delivered by Lord Porchester. It
was spoken in a very full House, at the
fullest time, about ten o'clock, and was received by the Conservatives with immense
applause. The speech was a very good
one in itself; it was against the Reform
Bill, a subject on which his father, Lord
Carnarvon, an old Whig, had separated
from his party, and it is not impossible

that this circumstance may have added to the vehemence of the cheers with which the son's oratory was welcomed. I remember thinking that such a success was worth years of life, and wondering whether I should ever achieve anything like it. I remained silent so long that some of the party rather reproached me, and said that it was expected of me to speak. The present Lord Mansfield, I remember, was of the number. At last I mustered courage and spoke shortly, and was very well received by both sides of the House. Hardinge, with whom I had very little acquaintance, gratified me by saying that the tone I had taken was exactly suited to the House of Commons, and as different as possible from what was usually adopted by lawyers. In short, I was greatly delighted with my performance; but on looking the next morning in the newspapers I found— what so many in the same circumstances have found—that my speech was hardly noticed. This is so common that I should scarcely have mentioned it, if it had not led to my next appearance in the House obtaining much more attention in the public press than it would probably otherwise have done. Poor Mackworth Praed, whose early death was a great loss to the country, thought that the neglect to report my first speech was so unfair that he took the trouble himself, as he afterwards told me, to report the second, and send it to the newspapers. It was on the second or third reading of the Reform Bill, I forget which, and acquired for me a good deal of credit.

There is nothing so intoxicating, I think, as the success of a speech in the House of Commons, and no effort of which the reward is so out of all proportion to the merit. A single speech of Wilde against me on the Privilege question made him Attorney-General, Chief-Justice of the Common Pleas, a Peer, and Chancellor. A single

H

speech of Cockburn's carried him to the
high office which he holds of Chief Justice
of the Queen's Bench.   I do not mean, of
course, that both these men were not
men of mark, who afterwards did very well
in Parliament, and very greatly at the
Bar; but the two speeches to which I
have alluded brought them into notice,
and into great reputation as debaters, and
but for them neither would probably have
attained any very high distinction.   One,
certainly, when he was raised to the Bench,
had not the credit of much knowledge of
law; and to both there were objections of
different kinds to their holding judicial
office, which nothing but strong political
claims could have surmounted.   My success was nothing of this kind.   I was already in a position at the Bar which made
my advancement to the Bench, if I
wished it, pretty secure; the principal difference which I felt was in the alteration
which it made in my social position, in

the introduction into society to which I had not been accustomed, and for which, in truth, I was not very fit. I had neither the animal spirits nor the conversational talents which make men popular in company, nor the easy indifference which an early familiarity with it is, perhaps, necessary to produce. I was always, and still remain, shy and taciturn, and like no place so well as my own chimney-corner.

In 1832 the Reform Bill was carried, and in the end of that year the Parliament was dissolved. I went down to offer myself as a candidate for Taunton, and was received by the populace with the favour which always attends a third man, that is, a man who both spends money himself, and is the cause that his opponents spend it also. After canvassing the place for two days, and spending about £800, I found that I had no chance, and came away, and from that time till the end of 1834 I remained out of the House. In the au-

tumn of 1834 the King turned out the
Ministers, and sent for the Duke of Wellington. Sir Robert Peel was at that time
on the Continent, and the Duke thought
that he ought to be at the head of the
Government. The Duke himself accepted
in the interim half-a-dozen offices, in order
that Peel might not be embarrassed by any
appointments. In a very short space of
time Peel returned, and undertook the
Government; he offered me the Solicitor-
Generalship, Lyndhurst being Chancellor,
and Pollock Attorney-General. Before he
returned I had been invited, at the sug-
gestion of Manners Sutton, the Speaker,
to go down as a candidate to Ripon,
which had been a close borough in the
hands of Mrs. Lawrence, the owner of
Studley. In consequence, however, of the
excitement of the Reform Bill, and the
grossly bad management of her agents,
under the superintendence, as it was said,
of Vice-Chancellor Shadwell, both her no-

minees had been defeated at the election
of 1832, one of them, Colonel Dalbiac,
being a candidate with me at the next
election. Mrs. Lawrence was said to be
so disgusted that she would not at all in-
terfere at the new election; and, as I went
down with my brother without any introduction, and nobody called upon us on
our arrival, the prospect looked black
enough. However, in the dusk of the
evening, as we were sitting after dinner, in
rather melancholy mood, at the Unicorn
Inn (one of the worst in England), the
Rev. Mr. Charnock, Mrs. Lawrence's do-
mestic chaplain, was announced, and he
told us that though, after the treatment
which she had received, Mrs. Lawrence
did not choose to take any ostensible
part, she was very desirous of the success
of Dalbiac and myself, and that, in fact,
one of her agents would go round with
me the next day on my canvass, and that
he had no doubt all her tenants would vote

for me; and so it turned out. Our adversary, Shirley, went to the Poll, but we were returned by a large majority.

The Solicitor-Generalship, on my declining it, was offered and accepted by Follett, who had acquired most deservedly a vast reputation at the Common Law Bar, and also before election committees. The seat at Ripon, I believe, had been offered to him before it was proposed to me, but he was engaged to stand for Exeter, of which place he was a native, and for which he was returned. Lord Lyndhurst, before Parliament met, offered me a puisne judgeship, which I declined, and Coleridge was appointed. For the judgeship I was totally disqualified; indeed, I had always a great distaste for judicial office, which I never hesitated to declare, and I have often since been reminded of it; and, though circumstances have placed me in a position in which now for above fifteen years I have been more or less occupied in the discharge of judicial duties, and have found them less irksome than I expected, I have never once regretted having declined the promotion to the Bench which at different periods has been offered to me.

The refusal of the office of Solicitor-General I cannot so well justify. My position at the Bar and my success in the House of Commons were sufficient to give me a reasonable assurance of discharging its duties with tolerable efficiency; and with the Attorney-General a common lawyer, and not a very powerful speaker in the House, the road to the Great Seal seemed open to me. I am afraid it was only a moral cowardice which occasioned my rejection of the offer. I announced the fact to Sir Robert Leigh in a very foolish letter, and I have no doubt, though he never said so, that he was greatly annoyed at it. He was anxious to have his property enjoyed and his family represented by some person of station; and he had selected me as his heir, principally because I seemed more likely than any other member of his family to fulfil this desire on his part; and now I had wilfully thrown away the chance, or almost the certainty, of having at least a Privy Councillor's office (for at that time the Vice-Chancellor was always a Privy Councillor) at my disposal. I had, apparently, "slunk from the course when that immortal garland is to be run for not without dust and heat," and doomed myself to voluntary obscurity; and Sir Robert might not un-naturally suppose that I had quitted the road to wealth and honour, in reliance on the rich inheritance which he had promised to leave me. I cannot help thinking that this circumstance was not without its weight in the alteration of his will, which he made some years afterwards. Yet so differently are the events of the world ordered, both in public and in private matters, from the expectations which are formed of them by the actors in them, that the very circumstance which seemed to exclude me from future distinction was probably the cause of my attaining a distinction which I believe was never before enjoyed by any other English barrister— that of being a Privy Councillor while I remained in practice at the Bar—that I was offered a peerage by four Governments in succession, and that by the last, Lord Derby's, the Great Seal was not only offered to me, but pressed upon my acceptance.

Though the Whig Government had begun to lose its popularity almost as soon as the Reform Bill had been carried, and had, indeed, been utterly shattered and broken to pieces by internal dissension, and by the retirement of several of its members, especially of Lord Stanley and Sir James Graham, and, finally, by the resignation of Lord Grey, and the substitution in his place of Lord Melbourne, before the end of 1834, yet it appeared on the election of 1835 that the dismissal of the Government had been premature and ill-judged, and that the new House would not support a Conservative administration. The question was first tried in a manner the most favourable to the Ministers, viz., on the choice of a Speaker, Charles Manners Sutton being proposed by Sir R. Peel, and Mr. Abercromby by the Opposition. Up to the time of going into the House the majority was supposed by our side to be quite certain in favour of Sutton; but, although Stanley and Graham joined us, Abercromby was elected by a majority of ten. Sutton was deeply mortified; it was said that tears were seen on his cheeks; he had insisted on one of the Opposition, who had promised his support in ignorance that the choice was to be made a party question, adhering to his promise, and the member got up and made this statement to the House. After this decisive proof of the temper of the majority, it was obviously impossible that the Government could maintain itself.

On the dismissal of the Melbourne Ministry, the King had sent to the Duke of Wellington. The dismissal was late at night. Lord Brougham, before the matter was known to his colleagues, sent to the 'Times' newspaper a paragraph announcing that the Government was out, that the Queen had done it all, and that the Duke of Wellington was with the King. The facts as to the dismissal and the conduct of Lord Brougham I had learned from Bickersteth; and I turned them to good account in a speech which I made on the Address, which was very well received. Peel struggled on through constant defeat in the House of Commons, but ill supported even by his own friends, who saw the hopelessness of the contest.

A meeting was called at Lord Francis Egerton's to endeavour to secure a better attendance; but in the following April Peel resigned, having, however, acquired an immense reputation with both sides of the House and with the country for the ability which he had displayed while conducting the business of the nation.

The most curious circumstance attending the entry upon office of the Tory Government was the conduct of the ' Times ' newspaper. It had been frantic on the subject of Reform, absolutely revolutionary in its language, had supported the Whigs throughout, and was supposed to be supplied not only with information but with articles by Lord Brougham. It seems that some quarrel had taken place, and a note was said to have been picked up in the Chancellor's private room, in Lincoln's Inn, which had been torn, but of which the fragments were put together, and easily legible to this effect: " Shall we

declare war against the ' Times ' or not?"
However this may be, the fact is that, instead of a furious article against the Duke
of Wellington accepting office on behalf
of Peel, a rather favourable opinion was
expressed of the change. Soon afterwards
Lord Hardinge, then Sir Henry, gave a
dinner to a large party of the House of
Commons, to introduce them to Mr.
Sterling, one of the principal editors of
the paper, a party of which I made one.

On the return of Lord Melbourne to
power, Lord Brougham was not restored
to the Chancellorship, to his extreme indignation, which he took every opportunity of venting in the House of Lords.
On one occasion Lord Melbourne observed that the noble and learned Lord
must be well aware that, with his great
powers as a debater, and the weight which
he possessed with a large party in the
country, every Administration must be
desirous of securing his services, if the

most decisive reasons to the contrary did not exist. I have often heard Lord Langdale observe that, after this rebuke, Lord Brougham always remained silent on the topic, as if allusion were made to something then secret, but which the Government might be provoked to disclose. I do not myself think that there was anything of the kind. Lord Brougham's extreme indiscretion in everything connected with the King while he was in office, and his scandalous behaviour to the Queen when he was turned out, were abundantly sufficient to induce the King to refuse to receive him.

There was considerable difference of opinion in the Cabinet, as I have heard from Lord Langdale, whether he or Pepys should be the new Chancellor; but the decision was in favour of Pepys, and my great friend and opponent became Master of the Rolls, with a peerage, which he told me he strongly objected to receive, but it was forced upon him. As a mere lawyer he was not equal to Pepys, who became Lord Cottenham, and was certainly, as long as I remained at the Bar, one of the best judges I ever saw on the Bench. But Lord Langdale would probably have made a better Chancellor as regards politics and legislation, though he did not make as much figure as a Speaker in the House of Lords as was expected. But he had a great fondness for law reform, a strong feeling in favour of popular rights, and at the same time a deep sense of the extreme importance of maintaining order and the supremacy of law, though he enjoyed a vast reputation amongst the Philosophical Radicals. With these qualifications, his appointment to the Chancellorship would certainly have been useful to the country, and of importance to the Government. Lord Cottenham had no showy qualities of any kind. The effect of the change from Brougham to Cottenham on the Prime Minister was well expressed by some one who remarked that Lord Melbourne must feel very much like a man "who had parted with a brilliant, capricious mistress, and married his housekeeper."

The promotion of Lord Langdale to the Bench left me without a rival in the Rolls Court, and in the House of Lords and the Judicial Committee I had, I think, as much business as any counsel at the Bar. Follett was usually either with me or against me in the Lords, and possessed an influence there which he did not always use very fairly. Independently of his great abilities and knowledge, and reputation in Parliament, he was by marriage a connection of Croker's, and from all these circumstances both Brougham and Lyndhurst treated him, I think, with some partiality. Sir Edward Sugden had been removed by taking the Great Seal of Ireland under Sir R. Peel's Government; so that a great opening had been made at the Bar. I must do Lord Cottenham the justice to say that I never found any leaning on his part to any counsel either from fear or favour; and, notwithstanding his strong political opinions, he treated both me and Follett with as much civility and paid as much attention to our arguments as if we had been of the same party with himself. Indeed, Lord Langdale told me that Lord Cottenham always expressed a strong opinion of our superiority to the other counsel who practised before him. We hear now much of the importance of a numerous Court in the Lords. In my opinion, the business there was never so well done as during the session in which Lord Cottenham sat alone, Lord Brougham being absent, from the death of his daughter.

I do not know that anything very material to me occurred as regards my professional and public life for three or four years after the establishment of the Mel-

bourne Government. My course at the
Bar was one of uninterrupted success, and
I took little or no part in the House of
Commons till the great question of Par-
liamentary Privilege arose in 1838.

In the various occasions on which this
question came before the House in the
following years I spoke several times, with
varying success, against what seemed to me
the monstrous pretensions of the House.
It was undoubtedly a question on which
the leaders of the Opposition—Peel, Stanley, and Graham—were quite as strong in
favour of Privilege as Lord John Russell
and the other members of the Government and the Radicals, so that the game
which we had to fight was a difficult one;
and Pollock and Follett (Peel's Attorney-
and Solicitor-General), though they could
not maintain the extravagant claims of the
Commons, had so far committed themselves that they did not like to speak
against them. One night when I sat down,

after speaking rather strongly on the subject, Peel said to me, "Pemberton, I do not complain of you at all for the course you are taking; you stated your views at the beginning; but I do complain grievously of my late law officers, who never told me that we were going too far till it was too late for the House to retrace its steps without disgrace." I had a good share in the arrangements which were afterwards made for settling the matter by Act of Parliament, against which the Radicals protested as in truth a surrender of the right. Perhaps at some time I may go more into detail in this matter.

In 1841, on Peel becoming Prime Minister, Lord Lyndhurst resumed the Great Seal, Sugden returned as Chancellor to Ireland, and Pollock and Follett took again their old offices. In November of that year, on the birth of the Prince of Wales, I accepted, on Peel's proposal, the office of his Attorney-General; and from the letter which I received from Sir Robert Leigh, expressive of his gratification on the occasion, I perceived how much he had been mortified by my rejection of other official situations. There was a salary of one hundred guineas a year attached to the office, which I foolishly declined, expecting, of course, that my fees would be properly marked and paid for all the business connected with the Law Department, in which I acted as counsel. Had this been done, the office would have been most inadequately paid, for I was made a member of the Council, and had in that character to attend not unfrequently for several hours together, for which I neither received nor expected to receive any remuneration. I did a great deal of work, drawing the scheme for the conduct of the business, prepared the Acts of Parliament for regulating the rights of the Prince, answered cases, and had various consultations on important matters, in

which, if my fees had been regularly
marked and paid by a private solicitor,
they could not, I think, have amounted
to less than £500. At the end of the
year I was informed by the Secretary that
the Council had voted me one hundred
guineas for my services. I was naturally
extremely indignant, and thought of sending them word that I had ordered the
money to be paid to my clerk. I let it
remain some time, but at last drew for it,
rather than produce a scandal. At the
Bar all questions of money are, or at least
used to be, thought beneath the dignity
of a barrister to mix himself up with;
but when I ceased to hold the office,
which I did almost immediately afterwards, I expressed to the Council very
strongly my opinion as to the improper
mode in which the Attorney-General was
treated.

In the latter end of December, 1842,
I received a summons to go down with

Mrs. Cooke to Hindley, where Sir Robert was lying dangerously ill, and not expecting to recover. We accordingly went down, and found him better than we had expected. His old fondness for classical quotation remained to the last. I remarked on the strength of his voice as a favourable sign. "No, Sir," he said, "it is 'vox nil mortale sonans.'" At this time I had not the least notion that he had made any alteration in his will; and though I had heard that he had, or imagined he had a natural son, it never occurred to me that it could make any difference in his testamentary dispositions, so lightly was he accustomed to treat connections of that description.

One afternoon, as I was sitting with him in his room with Mr. Gaskell, his attorney, he inquired of Gaskell whether he had told me of the alteration in his will. "No, Sir Robert," replied Gaskell, "you know you never would allow me to do so." "Well,

Sir," he said, "then tell him now, for I will not die under false colours." On leaving the room with Gaskell, he told me that in the spring of the year Sir Robert had agreed that he should have a grant for his life of the house in which he lived at Whitley, free from rent, in consideration of the money which he had laid out upon it, and that he would leave it to him by his will; that they came up together to London, and that while they were there Sir Robert had expressed his intention to leave his estates, after Mrs. Cooke's death and mine, to the boy whom he took for his son, and that the will had been drawn accordingly. This was rather a blow to me, though, as I was unmarried and not likely to marry, it did not so much matter. The next morning, when I saw Sir Robert, he said, "Well, Sir, has Mr. Gaskell told you what I have done?" And on my answering in the affirmative, he added, "And don't you think, Sir, that I have acted like a great scoundrel?" Of course I disclaimed any such opinion, and said that, as matters were, it did not signify much, but that if I had married in the confidence of the communication which he had made to me, and had, indeed, published to all the family and his acquaintance, the consequences would have been very serious. "Sir," he said, "the truth is, I thought that you never would marry, and that you would therefore never have any legitimate children; and I thought that my bastards had a better right to the estate than your bastards." In this I quite agreed, but observed that that was not the effect of the will, for that if I had legitimate children they would not succeed. After some further talk, he declared that he was satisfied that what he had done was not right, that it was leaving away a family estate from the family, and that his child might be amply provided for by a sum of money, and he desired me to draw up a codicil to give effect to his determination. I told him, of course, that this was quite impossible; that I could have no hand in the preparation of any instrument under which I was to take a benefit; and he then desired me to see Mr. Gaskell and send him to Hindley. At this time he was as much in possession of all his senses as I ever saw him. I went over to Wigan, and saw Gaskell, who could not or would not come at the time, but came either that afternoon or the next morning, and said that Sir Robert was not sufficiently collected to do so important an act. I saw him soon afterwards, and he certainly was wandering, but this is what I believe happens very commonly in a last sickness, that men's minds wander occasionally, though at other times they are quite masters of themselves. Gaskell, however, obviously did not like the job, and, instead of waiting till Sir Robert was more collected, or coming again on another day, he took no further steps in the matter, nor did I attempt to do so.

Sir Robert died after I had been obliged to return to town, in the month of January, 1843, upon which occasion of course I went down to Hindley, my aunt, Mrs. Cooke, having remained there till his death. On opening his will and codicils, it was found that he had left £20,000 as a provision for the boy till he came into possession of the estate; that the whole residue of the personalty, amounting, with the £20,000, to about £200,000, was to be laid out in land, and settled, with the estates, on Mrs. Cooke for life, with remainder to me for life, with remainder to the boy for life, with remainder to his first and other sons in tail male, with remainder to my first and other sons, with remainder to such uses as I should by will appoint.

Not long after the funeral Lord Bal-

carres undertook to take charge of the
boy. In my situation I could hardly do so.

Mrs. Cooke, with a liberality of which
I never knew such an instance, gave up
to me the whole of her life interest in the
estate, of which the income was not less
than £14,000 a year, and would not receive even an annuity out of it. I hope
that on the whole I showed my gratitude
and affection for her to the close of her
life, and yet my memory now reproaches
me with too many instances in which, had
I shown the same kindness to any of her
relations, I should have thought them
guilty of ingratitude and neglect.

I was now on the verge of fifty. I had
reached a position at the Bar beyond
which I could not rise without taking
office either political or judicial, and I had
no taste for either. I had a large income
for my life, and had accumulated some
£60,000 or £70,000, had no incum-
brance of natural children, and no incli-

nation to marry, and I determined to take a step which excited the surprise of most of my friends, and was, perhaps, a very hazardous one with a view to my happiness. I resolved to give up my seat in Parliament, the best and safest in the House, to leave the Bar, and spend the remainder of my life in ease and retirement as a country gentleman. The first thing I did with this view was to write to Sir Robert Peel, resigning my office of Attorney-General to the Prince, and placing the seat for Ripon at his disposal whenever he liked to fill it. I received a very kind and gratifying letter from him as regarded myself, expressing the earnest anxiety of the Queen and the Prince that I should not quit the service of the Prince of Wales, and that, as I had resolved to leave the Bar, and could no longer be Attorney-General, I would accept the office of Chancellor, which was then held by Prince Albert. I assented to this request, which I had no decent pretext for refusing, and received a note from Sir Robert expressing his gratification, and adding that my acceptance enabled him to offer me (without embarrassing himself with other claims) a dignity which he thought peculiarly suited to me, that of a Privy Councillor. I gladly accepted the offer which gave all I could want—a certain position in the country, without entailing any restraints or obligations. Not long afterwards Lord Lyndhurst expressed a wish that I should consent to be one of the two members of the Judicial Committee whom the Crown has the power to appoint, though they have not held judicial office. I agreed to this, whenever I should leave the Bar, the period for which I had not fixed. It was not, therefore, without great astonishment that when I was called into the Queen's presence to be sworn in as a Privy Councillor I found that I was at the same time appointed to be a member of the Judicial Committee. Sir Edward Ryan, who had returned from India, where he had been Chief Justice of Calcutta, was sworn in a Privy Councillor on the same day, and became one of the assessors of the Judicial Committee in Indian cases. He was sworn in before me, and is therefore entitled to precedence of me, or at least was so before my Peerage, but he always refused to take it.

I was very much vexed at this blunder, (of my being appointed prematurely a member of the Judicial Committee), not only because it deprived me of the power of practising in a court which I liked, and in which I had a good deal of business, but because it gave the appearance of my office of Privy Councillor having been conferred on me with reference to my sitting there, and creating, therefore, a claim upon my services accordingly. I was not long in receiving a letter from the clerk of the Council, by the desire of Lord Wharncliffe, then president, to inquire when I would take my seat at the Board. This gave me an opportunity, of which I availed myself, to explain the circumstances of my appointment, and to state that whenever I retired from the Bar I should be ready to take my seat as a member of the Judicial Committee.

In the meantime I continued to practise at the Rolls, and in the House of Lords, being, I believe, the only English barrister who ever during his continuance in practice held the rank of Privy Councillor. Tinney called me " the Great Commoner." In Ireland it is constantly the case, the Attorney-General of Ireland being always an Irish Privy Councillor. When Stuart Wortley some years afterwards, who was a Privy Councillor, having been Judge-Advocate, returned to the Bar, and wished to practise at the Judicial Committee, there was some question amongst the members whether he could be heard, and they consulted me, and we were ultimately satisfied that he could not practise before the Privy Council, being a member of that body.

In the spring of 1843 I gave up my seat for Ripon, and was succeeded by Smith, the Irish Attorney-General; and at Christmas, 1843, I took the decisive step of leaving the Bar and retiring into the country. I could not but feel some misgivings as to the manner in which I should bear so great a change, from uninterrupted labour and strife in law and politics to a life of idleness and obscurity; and I looked not without some apprehension to the long winter evenings which I should have to pass alone. I provided myself with microscopes, telescopes, painting implements, a chest of turners' tools, and I know not how many other resources against ennui, none of which I ever used; and after the lapse of seventeen years I can safely say

that I have never had one hour hang
heavy on me, nor felt anything but regret
at being called upon to forsake my solitude
in order to attend the sittings of the Judicial Committee or the Duchy Councils.

In February, 1844, I commenced my
attendance as a member of the Judicial
Committee, and sat there regularly for
some years. The business of the Duchy
was much more troublesome than I had
expected.

The only agreeable part of my Chancellorship to me was, that it brought me
into constant and intimate communication with Prince Albert. Sir Robert Peel,
when he introduced me to him in 1841,
said that I should find him one of the
most extraordinary young men I had ever
met with, and so it proved. His aptitude
for business was wonderful; the dullest
and most intricate matters did not escape
or weary his attention; his judgment was
very good; his readiness to listen to any

K

suggestions, though against his own opinion, was constant; and though I saw
his temper very often tried, yet in the
course of twenty years I never once saw
it disturbed, nor witnessed any signs of
impatience. There were other advantages
in being connected with the Court, which
probably most persons would have valued
more highly than I did, viz. being invited to all the principal Court parties,
and to dine at Buckingham Palace, and
pay visits at Windsor. I did not under-
value these things, for of course the honour was great, and on the whole they
were very agreeable, but of course attended with the restraint which in its nature
is inseparable from a Court, and which,
I believe, is greater in the English Court
than in any other, probably because in
this country the subjects are often more
powerful than the Sovereign. I was at
Windsor at the christening of the Prince
of Wales, which certainly was by far the

most splendid ceremony at which I was ever present. The King of Prussia was one of the godfathers, and he brought with him Humboldt, to whom I had the honour of being introduced. It was said that one hundred guests slept in the Castle that night. My room was in one of the towers at the further side of the quadrangle, and the Queen's carriages came to convey us at night to our quarters. On two occasions I went out shooting with the Prince, and other visitors, in one of which the Prince of Parma, who was afterwards murdered, was of the party. Prince Albert himself was, I think, the best shot I ever saw ; he scarcely ever missed. At one of the evening parties at Buckingham Palace I had the honour of being introduced to the French Emperor, whose countenance struck me as one of the most remarkable that I had ever seen, rather stern, very thoughtful, with a tinge of melancholy, but lighted up for a moment with a very sweet smile. The Empress did not seem to me as handsome as her reputation. The spectacle of two persons, both born in a private station, associating as Sovereigns with the descendant of a hundred kings on a footing of perfect equality, was very interesting.

* * * * * *

FINIS.

PRINTED BY J. E. TAYLOR AND CO.,
LITTLE QUEEN ST., LINCOLN'S INN FIELDS.